MISSING CHILDREN

BOOKS BY LYNN CROSBIE

POETRY

Miss Pamela's Mercy (1992)

VillainElle (1994)

Pearl (1996)

Queen Rat: New and Selected Poems (1998)

Missing Children (2003)

Phoebe 2002: An Essay in Verse (with Jeffery Conway and David Trinidad, 2003)

Liar (2006)

NOVELS

Paul's Case: The Kingston Letters (1997)

Dorothy L'Amour (1999)

ANTHOLOGIES

The Girl Wants To: Women's Representations of Sex and the Body (editor, 1993)

Plush: Selected Poems (editor, with Michael Holmes, 1995)

Click: Becoming Feminists (editor, 1997)

MISSING CHILDREN

LYNN CROSBIE

McCLELLAND & STEWART

Library and Archives Canada Cataloguing in Publication

Crosbie, Lynn, date
Missing children / Lynn Crosbie.

Poems.

ISBN 13: 978-0-7710-2425-2
ISBN 10: 0-7710-2425-8

1. Missing children – Poetry.   I. Title.

PS8555.R61166M59 2003   C811'.54   C2002-905227-0
PR9199.3.C6893M57 2003

We acknowledge the financial support of the Government of Canada through the Book Publishing Industry Development Program and that of the Government of Ontario through the Ontario Media Development Corporation's Ontario Book Initiative. We further acknowledge the support of the Canada Council for the Arts and the Ontario Arts Council for our publishing program.

Lyrics from "Born to Run" by Bruce Springsteen. Copyright © 1975 Bruce Springsteen (ASCAP). All rights reserved. Reprinted by permission.

Lyric from "I'm So Excited." Words and music by Trevor Lawrence, June Pointer, Ruth Pointer, and Anita Pointer. Copyright © 1982 EMI Blackwood Music Inc., 'Til Dawn Music, Anita Pointer Publishing, Ruth Pointer Publishing, and Leggs Four Publishing. All rights controlled and administered by EMI Blackwood Music Inc. All rights reserved. International copyright secured. Used by permission.

Detail of mitten on page i from a painting by Jennifer Febbraro.

Text design by Sean Tai
Typeset in Perpetua by M&S, Toronto
Printed and bound in Canada

McClelland & Stewart Ltd.
75 Sherbourne Street
Toronto, Ontario
M5A 2P9
www.mcclelland.com

9 10 11 12   14 13 12 11

For James Crosbie

...stories in the news this week that have been haunting me – one was one of the most sinister things I've ever seen. A guy somewhere in M— had been arrested, except they didn't quite know what to charge him with. For years he'd been collecting newspaper clippings about missing children and unsolved murders – then on the child's birthday or the anniversary of the murder, he would call the family of the victim and pretend to have vital information on the case or to know the child's whereabouts and say he would call and tell more. And then never call again.

– June 21, 2000

4 A.M.

A streak of tigers filing through mangrove swamps, dry thorn forests,
tall green grass.

One detaches from the palms.

His pupils dilate as he crouches low.
    A stag shifts in a bed of emerald needles
and turns.

There is a crush of orange and black
the blood courses through

Asia, India, and Siberia

tracking what predators remain.

I

The sound in their throats is *Kol Nidrei*

the deer, listening, are petrified –

⁎

I close my book and walk the floor, restless; slip away and pry the box from the shelf.

Sift through its newest contents: a lemon slice, checked Scrunchie, a necklace of bread clips, Hamburgler, a construction-paper fan trimmed with bow-tie pasta, a starry party hat.

Retrieve the mitten from its litter of tissue, red angora, a pendant string.

Something newborn, terrible.

A thin voice crying: I pitch it back, and seal the lid.

Lace my shoes and steal outside.

⁎

I hug the edge of the sidewalk
stick to dark wooded streets.

The moon is full and bright,
a wheel of cheese.

Tonight the street narrows
and declines,

there is a formation,
two rows of pine

bearing white flags.

Advancing, I see the sheets of paper
stapled there:

Another child is missing.

Two Birds

She left the house after midnight, running barefoot
her dressing gown parted, lifting like tail feathers.
And slid into the car beside me on the bench seat with two pillowcases
spilling sheer white and violets. Smoothing her wet black hair,
she looked at me evenly and took my hand.

Crow on a trembling branch.

The sky was hemmed with lavender, straight-pinned with stars.
In this silver light I looked back and saw the little one start down the
road after her.

His cowboy pyjamas billowing, he canters,
legs unsteady lariats, his arms raised.

She saw him too. Glancing in the rear-view mirror,
she pressed my knee and we accelerated, coughing up gravel and stones.

I think he was hit, the way he fell down and cried out,
brown spurs revolving against red,

nightingale.

The Edgewater

When she started waitressing at the Edgewater,
I would sit in her section entire afternoons and into the night
trying to catch her attention.

A regatta of lemon slices with toothpick masts and furled Cellophane sails
cruised through the draft, sluicing from glasses I ordered four at a time.

Tips folded into petals, blue carnations, salt and sugar spelling out her name.
Finally she wiped my table clean, and wrung the towel over my lap.

Starlets falling, she laughed with her head thrown back,
her hair licking the tiers of bottles, filled with pale gold.

GULLS

The bar overlooks one of the five Great Lakes.
Its patio narrows like a rifle into a wooden pier.

I wasn't looking to meet anyone – I liked the time alone to write
in my notebook, some lists I was making,

letters I was working on, the odd poem.

I was on disability: at my last job, a janitor in an elementary school, I
slipped on a floor I had just waxed, causing back injuries too arcane
to diagnose or treat, a hairline skull fracture that led to *debilitating
migraines*.

I copied out my injuries for my lawyer, including a shin splint
and aggravated fibromyalgia: a devastating and perplexing condition.

She was talking on the pay phone to one of her children when I first
noticed her, hissing at the child to Stop crying or I'll give you something
to cry about.

She flushed when she noticed me watching; I closed my notebook.

The first of the gulls assembled on the pier, diving for fish and garbage

JEWEL

She wore a wedding band, a sapphire ring she said her husband
    Wrenched off his mother's hand.
I had stopped working altogether, followed her shifts like a shadow,
    never speaking.
She asked if I was sleeping, passed her hand over my eyes.
Clasping it, I worked the rings from her fourth finger and swallowed,
    biting hard –

The impression of my teeth there, a band of opals.

Geometry

I began to think of elemental shapes, circular motions reproduced in nature; the corners of a square; the triangle her husband completed.

Wendy and Lew lived in an apartment off the Lakeshore. They had four children, aged three through seven.

Lew sold scrap metal, lengths of pipe, aluminum flanges. His business card read: *I Meat You're Needs*.

I asked Wendy, sincerely, if he was retarded.

He's not so bad, she said, defensively. I know she is remembering something I can never know:

her body a downy, heavy pear, curving toward him in sleep; Lew reaching for her, his piebald face opening,

a giraffe wresting pears from a tree.

INTIMATION

She put down her scissors and kissed me,
her mouth flowering like a sliced radish in water,

her papers sledding off the bar.

I thought she saved coupons, but later
discovered she was collecting

what she called Sad stories about
the elderly.

She had filled a shoebox already.
I'm thinking of writing a book, she said.

She kept her favourites in her wallet,
folded over like moist towelettes.

An old man who wandered into a cow pasture
dressed like a toreador.

A lady whose own
children tied her to a radiator.

A kind of a gang, arrested for stealing
canned goods and "one large eggplant."

The one who died in the blizzard.
Someone fixed his head with a carrot and coal.

I know it isn't funny, she said about the last,

her face in her sleeve.

It's terrible, what happens to some people.

Passionata

Clinches in the storeroom
between fifty-pound bags of flour,
barrels of oil and lard;

latching onto her beside the pool table,
her hands are chalked blue.

I followed her into the ladies' room
and mauled her by the sink

among the lipsticked tissue
and snarls of hair,

a matchbook with raised letters –
Where the Elite Meet to Eat –

all but two matches torn out.

I took the cue to bite her neck.

She wore a lot of scarves back then,
turtlenecks, Elastoplast.

The Count, she called me.
Her husband was *That Fatso*.

It was weeks before she said yes.

I took her to the bird sanctuary and pressed
her hand against my fly. I'm going crazy, I said

She kept tossing breadcrumbs,
her face bright red.

This duck waddled over and bit her
from behind.

She cried and jumped up, lifted her skirt.

The bill had left a green mark, some scarlet
spreading where I planted my mouth.

Two teenage boys said Get a room —

The geese moved in formation, heading south.

I reserved a room at the Mancanza;
registered us as Mr. and Mrs. Hart.

I arrived early and lowered the blinds,
washed up with a pink seashell.

She was a little unsteady, walking in.
I went to hug her and she shrugged me off,

flicked her fingers at the satin
lampshade and bedspread.

The *Mancanza*, she said, her lip curled.

She slid down the wall and closed her eyes:
I've never done this before.

Someone in the next room was yelling,
You always get the good underwear!

The room shook when traffic passed.
I righted the picture above the bed, and drew her in beside me.

Two black pintos, rearing against an orange sky.

SAFE

I began bringing her home.
The hotel was too risky,

she was imagining private eyes
casing the room,

nights of surveillance, shutters
releasing like castanets.

She gave me a poster for my bedroom,
something called *Love Is* she picked up at the flea market.

A naked, dwarfish couple hand in hand,
declaring that love involves sunshine on rainy days.

I'm freckling, I told her, as the bed squeaked.

I pulled away precipitously, broke the safe,
and pulled it off in gaudy pieces --

Glo-Latex Ribbed for Her Pleasure.

I wouldn't mind having children.

I got four already, she said.
And two stillborn, one miscarriage.

The fertile Nile Delta, I said,
hooking her legs over my shoulders.

Think of some baby names, I told her
and she screwed up her face, thinking hard.

Bounce, she said. And Princess.

Names I heard the lady next door calling after her cats.

I would go through her purse one day.
And find spermicide jelly, sponges, a cookie-sized
diaphragm.

Open and close the clasp, remembering.

Gold flocked wallpaper, the golden light in her hair
through the crook in my arm,

Wendy nestled there.

I feel safe, she said.

WATER

I don't want to talk about them any more, she said,
turning away and reaching for her hairbrush.

You look like a painting, I said, like the girl in the basin.
She looks like a bitch too.

Wendy pitched her brush at me, recited
Charlie, Hannah, Jeff, and Lily.

She didn't carry pictures.
I asked what her husband was like.

He hits me, she said, and I believed her.

Madeleine Finch, age 5, has been missing since August
She was last seen riding her bicycle by the ravine.
She has blonde hair and blue eyes.
She was wearing a white T-shirt and shorts.

I am composing the letter in my head:

Your daughter is near the woods, I see her
when I close my eyes –

Beneath the pine boughs, a spike of moonlight.

EROSION

It is easier than you think, something like the way water
shapes stones.

She becomes sharp with me, asks how I'd like it,
ribs broken, bruises like the aurora borealis.

I would never lay a finger on you, I tell her, smoothing away
her frown, the edges of hand and elbow, bound in anger.

I tell her she can stop working, I will take care of her.
She turns and her face is pink with pleasure,

a stone I saw underwater.

I was underwater, and could not breathe.

I pick up the paper every morning and read
around what she has cut out.

Children gone missing. It begins to feel like an
epidemic.

Look up addresses and print slowly,
Dear Mr. and Mrs. Jay,

You don't know me, but –

Dear Mr. and Mrs. Jay,

You don't know me, but I was so sad to read about Jess.
I lost a girl of my own when she disappeared on a camping trip.
I am still afraid of bears, tall trees, and pup tents.
She may have drowned, there was a river there.
It had a fast current, I saw leaves and twigs getting mangled.
My girl was also named Jess.
Her hair was light and always tangled; she slept in her departed
    mother's slip.
May the Good Lord bless you,

Sorrowfully —

JEALOUSY

Wendy and I were lovesick, occupied with making plans.
I would kill someone for looking at you, she said.

She is braiding her hair, cross-legged, on my bed.
Who would look at me? I ask.

She crawls toward me, and cradles my head:
her long nails rake my scalp.

Some whore called while you were out, she says,
her lips compressed, unleavened bread.

I raise my hand, and catch myself; unravel her hair instead.

She asks who called, brushing her teeth like she is
going after shower mildew.

She sounds about ten years old, she says.

Working the floss like a saw; her tongue jumps,
making way.

I mean to tell her not to be jealous, that it was my second cousin,
someone.

19

I mean to say these things, and cannot.

Her suspicions, an architecture, frighten me.

KITCHEN

She leaves me pot pies, casseroles in labelled Ziploc
containers, with careful instructions:

You may think it's safe to eat, but it will be *too hot*.

Make sure to handle this with pot holders, the steam is also dangerous.

Do not feed this to your dog.

Jennifer, my old beagle, samples each dish.

Watch out she don't pizen you, I tell her, sounding something like
Tex Ritter in a movie about decent varmints and black-hearted saloon
girls.

Jennifer is retrieving her squeak toys:
hot dog, carrot, Mr. T-Bone, and mauling them, growling.

Wendy tells me she is allergic to animals.

It makes it hard for me to breathe, she says.

I watch Jennifer's frog legs as she scuttles under the chair,
think about her running on a farm.

Running until she tires; the farmer's whistle
calling her to a rough country dinner.

He whittles down a switch of birch and calls her Lady.

Dogs like the country, I concede.

Wendy says we could drive up and leave her there.

I had to start keeping her outside.
Afflicted with mange, she took to chewing at her raw skin.

She was wearing one of those plastic neck cones
when she chewed through the rope.

Ran right under the wheels of a truck;
the driver said she sounded like a bird.

He looked like he had been crying.

I remembered when I first found her.
She had been beaten; her legs were broken.

How could someone do this.

She sounded like a bird when she was dying.

LANAI

My basement apartment connects – with seven concrete steps –
to a converted garage with a line of windows

overlooking an oblong of asphalt and brick
Wendy likes to call *the lanai*.

Wendy convinced Billy, who owns the house,
to pay for some cleaning and garden supplies,

an old orange lawnmower with red blades.

She planted boxes of tomatoes, basil, and marigolds,
sanded and primed some patio furniture she found in the shed,

painted the chairs and table marmalade.

A warm breeze scatters leaves from the apple tree;
Wendy is setting out wine and water crackers, a small, round cheese.

A leaf decants and lands between us.
I tell Wendy that my dog was once this small.

She trusted me, I say.
Wendy lowers her head and looks away.

STUDIO

I still keep an office, although I haven't worked there in years.

The folders are still fanned across the desk, labelled

OLD, NEW, SENT, REJECTED, ACCEPTED.

The last is empty –

I wrote love poems using the name Louise Lamour,
sent them to magazines like *True Romance* and *True Confessions*.

My cover letter would indicate that attached were several
"songs of my heart."

Alone here at night I can hear Billy upstairs singing
himself to sleep.

One night, he got stuck on the words to "Best of Intentions";
he was cursing a blue streak while I rifled through some of the
old poems,

underlining the phrase that repeats like a chorus,
Where have you gone?

BATHROOM

She takes a bath every night after work, lines the ledge
with movie magazines, an ashtray, loofah, and glass of gin, neat.

Like a rat in her nest,

eating cheese and crackers or Fig Newtons, heedless
of the crumbs rising to the top of the water,

flecks of tobacco, soap scum.

It says here that when Elizabeth Taylor was a child, she ran away from
home, she tells me, folding over the page with one wet paw.

She packed all of her dolls and a jar of caviar into a Hermès case,
and walked to the end of her driveway screeching, I want a pony!

Her mother "carried the distressed child back to her room, and fed her
her favourite dinner: pork chops and apple sauce."

Wendy scowls and slides underwater.

I consider her black hair and milky skin, her violet eyes blazing
with anger and need,

fleetingly hold her head down and watch its ingress.
She is beautiful this way, soundless;

her hair spreading like the flukes of an anchor.

LIVING ROOM

The living room is attached to the bedroom (a box spring and mattress
enclosed by shelves and drywall).

The bank of sunlight uncovers strata of glittering dust.

Ulcerated velvet furniture I salvaged, meaning to re-upholster; tasselled
bordello lamps; a low, scarred wooden table.

My mother's Royal Doulton figurines gathered there – the fisherman;
derelict on a park bench; the balloon man; pale-blue praying children.

Don't touch them, ever.

Her censure precipitating obscure bouts of crying and door-slamming,
the occasional whimper, or peculiar request: *Get me some milk with ice
and lemon.*

I am dusting the figurines and berating myself: I am certain to break them.

Her words stick with me, like a leather bit and a set of spurs,
driving me to do better.

FINDINGS

I drew a diagram for the police. They became interested in the study, and tossed it, bagging pens and paper, glue and X-Acto knife, various illustrative tools, newspapers and magazines, maps, geometry set, an atlas.

They dragged off my computer as well, a selection of War Amputee stamps, stickers, my rhyming dictionary, each of my folders.

The box was hidden in the bathroom: it appeared to contain Stayfree Maxi Pads, with Wings.

This is how it started: I began to notice things that had been mislaid, or lost: pink barrettes, crayon drawings, running shoes;

once, an action figure rolled up in a bad report card, his head missing, fine thread binding his jackknifed legs; entreating arms.

I assumed the children would follow, and had started
making bunk beds, anchoring the frames to the wall with
L-brackets and butterfly clamps.

The night Wendy escaped, we crawled into bed and stayed there,
making the occasional incursion to wash or prepare hurried
snacks —

saltines and anchovies, celery mortared with cream cheese,
tangerines.

Do you miss them? I asked, snaking around her viscous thighs.

I haven't raised my hand in days, she said. That doesn't feel
right.

≫

Dear Mr. Lavender,

You do not know me but I have seen your child Olivia,
and want to tell you where she is, but I am afraid.

The man who has her keeps wild dogs in a pen
behind his shack and uses a shotgun –

I have come across the bodies of squirrels and worse,
there was a Scottie in a velvet tam-o'-shanter and cape.

He shouts at her to be a good girl: I drown him out
with heavy metal and a chainsaw.

I am not a bad person!

I want to tell you so much.

Your friend —

ACCESS

I contented myself for a long time being a stepfather of some kind;
I would stand at Lew's door and listen to him rage and curse,

hang my head and examine the extra holes he had carved in his belt
with what must have been a ballpoint pen.

That man could join the circus, I told Wendy.

I swear to you, he should be forklifted away from those children,
and returned to his goddamn pod.

Like you're perfect, she huffed, stamping away.

I checked myself out in the mirror; I looked all right, thin and sinewy,
smooth as a wrangler at a line dance.

Not a real man. I had been sticking her diaphragm with pins for months,
and she just kept getting thinner.

I thought about Lew with bitter envy, as if his fat concealed an arsenal
of heat-seeking missiles,

impervious to climate or radar, launched with the artless certainty
of a five-star general.

When she would carry on about being lonely,
I would drive her to Lew's and watch from the car.

The older children were diffident as she ruffled their hair; excited,
the little ones pulled at her legs like a wishbone.

She would hand them presents I had picked up at Wal-Mart,
six-shooters, paratroopers, sulky baby dolls,

call them her poor lost lambs.

Each time, like clockwork, I watched her eyes begin to dart,
her feet jerk, involuntarily, with boredom.

She would shake them off, and bark at them, Where's your father?

Fly through the door like a hornet, swearing to find him
and all that money he ate.

Lily came to the car one time and threw her dress over her head.

My pants have ducks, she yelled.

I reached out to touch her russet hair, tousled as a pile of leaves.

Wendy appeared in a flash and screwed up her face, bawling,
She's not your little girl!

I carried her into the car and reversed, holding her close as Lily began turning cartwheels.

Orange chevrons, a streak of white feathers.

ILLNESS

Wendy said she was sorry:
I feel so sick and I need you to take care of me.

I'm your little girl, she said; her skin was hot and damp,
the colour of parchment.

I had a shaky old doctor come in from MediVisit.
It's Demerol you really want, he said,

his voice shot through with half-remembered reprisals,
persistent deceptions.

I read where a man your age was stabbed for his black bag, she said.
And all he had in it was Aspirin and a stethoscope.

You're a nice woman, he said, aimlessly applying small plasters
to her chest, and whistling like a wood thrush.

I was delirious, when I wrote that card:

Dear Mrs. and Mr. Nightingale,

It is with joy that I convey to you my message from Jesus,
Who hath Plucked your child Susan from the Earth so that her
Suffering may cease forever in His healing Hands.

The messenger of the Light and the Life —

I sat beside her on the bed and watched her cold stretch into pneumonia
lapsing into sleep, I dreamed of bronchial trees

listing like spoiled broccoli, each floret
passing white light into the alveoli, irradiating

her breath – she is breathing like a dragon against my back.
I detach myself and prowl the kitchen, preparing a plate
of cold macaroni and Egg Foo Young.

I snap open a cookie and read in the moonlight that I

> *Will receive good news in a letter.*

She begins to sleep all day and night.
When she wakes up there are presents.

After Eights and Je Reviens,
a green scarf she looks like a peapod in.

I use my protractor to circle various points
of the mountain range where a girl named Callie Grackle slipped,

from the highest point to the lowest, impaling herself
on an urchin of rocks.

I thought she was dying.

32

She rattled, uncoiling herself from the mossy sheets.

I thought she was dying, Mr. Grackle.

The wolves picked up her scent and began circling:
their claws piercing the ice to break the trail;

ears pricked, wind lashing their pitched tails.

Where I Have Been

I was out walking when her fever broke.
At four or so, my shadow in the streetlight is long and narrow;

seedpods fall, revolving, to the ground.

I am trying to remember where I have been:
on another street, where lightning hit a girl in a short dress.

Her skin was branded with daisies.

A jacquard print that Wendy favours, the few nights we have
dinner somewhere ritzy,

followed by dancing: she spins in and out of my arms
until she is faint.

That girl was not hit by lightning exactly.

I would like the Dover Sole, Wendy states in a little voice,
and squeaks when it arrives

garnished with red petals, a Valentine.

Someone has dropped a box outside the window:
there is a whirl of white packing peanuts,

Like a hailstorm, she says.

She said she wanted to go home.

It wasn't really daisies, or a dress.

I don't remember what she wore, her cheeks were like poppies.

Wendy slaps my face, playfully.

You were miles away.

She wouldn't be quiet and her face was cold.

I have stood on a cold street, picking flowers.

PUMPKIN

She is soon her old self, spiking her morning coffee with chocolate
liqueur, steering her scissors through the newspaper.

I found a good one, she tells me. This lady has a pumpkin patch
the city wants to tear up and rezone.

These *pimpkins* are my babies, she told them.

Wendy considers laminating this one: It's a hall of famer, she says.

My hand shakes when I pass the sugar; she asks if I am ill,
and I don't answer.

I am fairly itching to get to my office and lock the door.

Black and orange markers, construction paper – green felt
for the patch I want to call HEAVEN,

the stems guarding the fontanelles, pooling into HALOS.

DOVE

Tell me about when you fell in love with me, she says,
putting her magazine aside.

She is having another bubble bath: I had come in looking for the
Palmolive.

I ran out of the salt and those beads, she complains.

She likes to melt them in her navel, and pick at the limp shell.

The water is scalding and she is bright red, Saturn in her rings
of gelatin and dirt.

I watch her magazine begin to curl, the girl on the cover is wearing
a shrimp-pink angora sweater.

You were over by the rose bush, I improvise. Shearing the branches
back.

She smiles, and I think she should know better.

The first time I saw her sleeping, she was in a spiral.
Her fingers splitting her lips, her black braids vertical, coming undone.

       Wendy tended to linger in *the powder room*,
       "polishing the chrome."

She loves euphemisms, for body parts and their functions,
things I would like to forget:

Backward Bingeing; Running with the Devil;
The Shining.

I would see her off after picking lint and wool nits
from her black skirt and apron,

using a quilted square of Shout on the cuffs and collar
of her white blouse,

and unscuffing her pumps with a spritz of vinegar.

She would squirm and tell me, I look fine, *Mother*.

If I sulked, and once I managed to cry, she would fall all
over herself: What would I do without you, I would be los
without you.

She might serve an important patron with a streamer
of toilet paper dragging off her shoe;

wear laddered pantyhose; or smile, revealing teeth glazed
with lipstick.

It is important that I stay on top of her, the things she does.

The bathroom after she has left —

a farrago of blackened towels, the washcloths also
a pen of skunks.

Toothpaste dried in the basin like bakery roses;
powder frosting the sodden tiles and mat, a cherry gateau.

Coarse black hair caked in the soap-dish,
veining the bar of Dove –

pared down to a thin slice, the writing
feathered,

I notice that it looks like Love when I am
scraping off the letters.

Chintz curtains, saffron and black;
a shelf for shower gels, a conch shell,

a row of paperbacks –

Tigers and Their Kin, *Heidi*, an old British series
about a sepulchral detective named Quill

and his Mandarin associate, Pang.

The librarian was throwing them out,
The last, she said, those mysteries are okay. I liked *Ghost Town*
the one about the Yukon.

Pang wears snowshoes and a parka.

Those others are kiddie books, let them alone.

The librarian was a heavy gal, shaped like a fir tree.
Her nose whistled when she was excited.

The time I heard her whispering about the police
asking questions, before they arrested me

on those charges that were later dropped.

I had the books with me, where I was.

The guy in the bed below me asked if I liked big cats:
I could feel him smiling, in the dark.

I found out my cellmate could barely read. His prison tattoo
was a heart with a MORON banner: he never knew.

The food they gave us tasted like paste and castor oil.

I began reading out loud to him, about tigers
lounging on the hills, stripping meat from hooves and claws.

Heidi in the Alps, her sullen grandfather making her a plate of
bread and goat cheese.

She is starving and the food fills her like helium.

I reread this passage over and over, until it sounds like a bell.

I keep the mysteries to myself.

This Quill character, he is forever changing his identity.
In Switzerland, he will be George, an investment banker;
in Athens, Auberon, an ivory dealer and card shark.

Pang is always the same.

The books made me uncomfortable:

I was once a cable television executive, and had a family of my own.

TWO

I found this place on a map, far east of where I lived last, after I was
let out.

I'd lived west of there before, and farther still when I was working for
Channel 4, The Family Station.

We had a big house in the east end; the two boys came after the
beagle pup, before my wife Gloria had her tubes tied "once and for all."

Ike and Kyle were short and squat, like tiny linebackers.

They liked to hide when you were coming up stairs, or carrying
something hot, then scream blue murder.

Stuff Jennifer in a pillowcase and toss her from the window.

Set fires in the basement and make explosives;
hunt cats with BB guns.

Read me a story, Kyle would say. Then Ike would sit in and improvise:

And then the Handsome Prince threw up all over Snow White and she
died. The End.

They pummelled me with their little fists when they laughed,
called out for me using variations on the word *stupid*.

Get me some water, retard!

I would cover my ears with the pillow, while Gloria adjusted her
sleep-mask.

I told you girls were less trouble, she said.

I began working nights, after Gloria became more
slovenly, then angry.

Standing in the kitchen up to her ankles in Tonka toys,
she hikes up the skirt of her robe and kicks a yellow
    bulldozer, hard.

It glances off my ankle, and I back away – she is thin and
sinewy, with eyes like a junkyard dog's.

I'll castrate you in your sleep! she growls.

I begin throwing 5mg Valium like Snausages.

She slumps down on a kitchen chair, buries her head in
her arms and cries.

Good girl, I tell her, let it all out.

I can't remember what she was mad about.
Someone had tacked up a MISSING CHILDREN flyer
to the bulletin board in the coffee room.

Warming my mouth on a cup of Nescafé, I ambled over –

Ellie Darling-Tanager
was last seen on Main Street.

She is two years old, and missing three teeth.
She is wearing a red elf costume.
Her shoes are felt and pointed.
She is friendly to strangers.

Please —

I thought of something; I thought of something else.
Discovering the elf in a tree trunk, her arms circling my neck.

    Hiding from my mother in the laundry basket.
    She is coming closer, smacking a wooden spoon against her
    thigh,

    telling me quietly to come out.

    She is too quiet: I bury my head in a mass of red delicates.

Her head, in its hood, is so delicate; the leaves beneath us crackle
like eggshell.

PINK LADIES

I began in the mailroom and worked my way up. Gloria worked as a
filing clerk for my boss, Mr. Purdue.

When I became a junior exec., I asked her out to dinner.

The Rampion is Redbird's finest restaurant. I made reservations weeks in
advance, slipped the captain a sawbuck for seats near the stage.

Gloria was a little on the frosty side, but she warmed up drinking
Pink Ladies.

She never touched the antipasto, the seeded rolls nesting in
white linen, the mint-sprigged cucumber soup.

Ignored her entree – rack of lamb with rosemary – and mooned over
the headliner, Denis Presley, a Cajun singer who loathed Elvis and his music.

He hissed imprecations from the apron when one diner called out
"Flaming Star!"

Holding the mic like a bayonet, he launched into a violent rendition
of Edith Piaf's "Boulevard du Crime."

Gloria asked me to dance, and I let her lead me to the floor.

The diners were restless; someone threw a salt shaker, wadded napkins.

Denis's children looked anxiously from behind the curtain,
twin girls in pink taffeta, their long black hair braided into coronets.

I stormed over to the heckler, forced him to his feet, and crab-walked
him outside. Gloria followed in stocking feet, her stilettos in her hand.

Later, she told me she wanted to see me again.
I pleated the tablecloth, making small rustling skirts.

We were lying in a heap on her single bed when a plan
came to me, as clear as a holy vision.

What if we started broadcasting MISSING CHILDREN posters?
And then updated them, using modern technology?

It would be like an electronic milk carton, I said,
fitting myself against her like a puzzle piece.

Gloria was impressed. Mr. Purdue will love that, she said
He told me the other morning he was just sick about that
Tanager girl.

Maybe he's the one who kidnapped her, I said.

She starts to say something, stops. She is thirty-seven
years old with skin like rawhide, and is an aunt twenty
times over.

I'll fix the coffee, she says. Using the comforter as a
makeshift toga, she pads away.

❧

My boss loved the idea and promoted me on the spot.

There was a flurry of publicity: I appeared on the radio and was quoted
in the paper saying that "At Channel 4, children matter."

After the initial excitement my idea bottlenecked: upper management
did not want to spend the money on computer enhancements;

the best artist in the field lived two counties over and was a notorious
double-biller and worse.

I volunteered to do the work myself and Mr. Purdue, who kept a flask
in his desk, agreed.

Remember that they will look different and somehow the same, he said.

My first two paintings appeared between episodes of *Full House*
and *Who's the Boss?* —

Ellie Darling-Tanager Imagined as Boticelli's Venus;
            Alexandra Waxbill in the Guise of Rembrandt's Danaë.

A crawl of text accompanied the images, cribbed from art books:

    Ellie's hair has grown to her knees and flows in rich carmine
    waves, which in addition to the swell of her hip, suggests fertility.

47

The tapestry extended to her by her attendant indicates a tension between modesty and immodesty;

her fine, intelligent eyes transfix the viewer.

A gust of pink flowers levitate beside her; she may be standing on the lip of a clamshell, surfing the Ionian Sea, or the banks of the Cumberland.

The aesthetics of her "outline" speak to certain "Florentine tendencies": her demeanour may be "deliberately archaic."

Alexandra awaits you as a GOD: you may come to her
in a rush of wings, a shower of coins, a shaft of golden light.

There is an "anguished cupid" who guards her every movement:
he is easily deceived by chicanery.

The golden light will spread across her braceleted arms
and illuminate her joyous face.

Her hair is now worn in a circlet at her crown; her belly is soft and yielding.

"[Her] naked body will seem to retain the impress of clothes" –
a mauve jumper and white turtleneck, patent-leather Mary Janes.

Please call —

When viewers were able to decipher what I had written,
they phoned the station, confused and outraged.

Sarah at reception logged more than one hundred calls that first
morning.

Some of them say they like the paintings, she said, uneasily.
This one call though . . .

Mr. and Mrs. Waxbill had asked for me.

Under "Message" on the slip were a series of numbers,
telephone, address.

I was at their door in fifteen minutes, taking deep breaths.

A large, stone-faced man answered; his wife, in a sequined
sweater, hovered at his elbow, swaying back and forth.

If I could see her room, I might be able to –

He held up his hand, and I stopped speaking.

Our girl was just five years old when she disappeared, he said.
She had guinea pigs – all dead now – she dressed in hats and
shawls.

She hated ice cream and loved spinach; after she had an
appendectomy, she would only speak to my wife and me in a
  whisper.

His wife's sweater says LEXY.

In this little whisper, she said to me
Don't leave me again.

As I am staring at the sweater I see stars.

The police are scraping me off the porch,
asking do I want to press charges?

I am too happy to answer. I have felt something exquisite and
rare as the talons of an eagle, a hatchling's mandible —

like white millet on the grass, there are sequins there.

Mr. Purdue said he wanted to keep me on, but They've got me by the
balls, son. He gave me a generous settlement package; we had a seven-
martini lunch and he introduced me to Nate the bartender as My boy.

He gave me a reproduction of J. E. H. MacDonald's *A Sandy Beach, Lake
  Ontario.*

I thought you could use this, he said. My son Jamie ran away
over ten years ago.

The desolation of the beach is mitigated by the Impressionistic rendering of the horizon,

the large scrub tree in the foreground that waxes with the moon.

I will not forget you, he said, and squeezed my leg a little too long.

The look in his eyes: "the light of one continent to another."

RETENTION

It isn't what you think.

My attorney, Jake Heifetz, and I are making a hairpin turn:
I cleave to the door of his silver Mercedes, straining at the shoulder
  harness.

He takes me to a fine steak house downtown, and orders
lobster salad and a twelve-ounce sirloin, rare.

I am too nervous to eat.

Those men you represent, I tell him, making a row of bread pills.

They're dangerous, sick.

Jake is an austere and daunting man; he smiles at me with large,
  incongruous lips –

I think of Hugo, Man of a Thousand Faces.

His accessories, the tiny spectacles and wigs; moustaches and various
  scars.

There was a Beatnik getup, goatee and Caesar-hair, designed to make
him seem affable and hip.

I hoist my martini and choke on the olive, recite: "who vanished into
nowhere . . . leaving a trail of ambiguous picture postcards."

Drumming the underside of the table with my knees.

Jake is impervious. He covers his bloodied plate with a napkin, signals for coffee.

Yes, the postcards, he says. We should talk about that.

Red Mitten

The single red mitten lay on top of the contents of the box,
a dead robin in its bower –

A small puddle, filled with one enormous fungus.

What I have seen on my street:

blue pipe cleaner; tissue flowers; two one-eyed Jacks; a computer's
ESC key; silver lettering on blue paper, SUMMER.

Mylar balloons levitating toward the hydro lines.
A sturdy boy in a GAP T-shirt racing toward them, yelling, No!

Heartbroken, a child's red mitten misplaced in snow.

Reaching to extract it from the drift, I feel the chilblains on her hand,
her hand is livid with cold.

        I was bent over a snowbank, when the storm began.

Placing the mitten over my tongue and closing my teeth.

        There is an impression of pink, where it has been.

There were seven picture postcards, seven representations
of the mitten in its caul of snow –

gouache, oil, egg tempera, and acrylic on canvas;

pastel, ink, and chalk on watercolour paper.

The subject modified in stages, from photo-realism to an abstraction,
entitled RED + WHITE (a brush pulled lightly across the surface,

its broken stroke is the *idea* of a mitten).

The messages were all the same:

It has been a year since — went missing.
I blame myself.

I blamed myself, I told Jake.

I could have loved them better.

LINE OF SCRIMMAGE

I worked about ten different jobs after I got laid off, often lying about my experience and skills.

They caught on fast at the clinics, and I lost my Echocardiographer and Kinesiologist positions quickly.

I lasted a while as a Receptionist for a Busy Hair Salon:
Steve, my boss, enjoyed my stories.

Tell me about that trip to Africa again while I sew on these extensions

I let the machine pick up and told him about the time I saw a giraffe walk her calf across the road;

baby gorillas saluting each other in semaphore from the acacia trees;

an abandoned lion cub facing a pack of hyenas at dusk.

Steve bends over the girl's scalp, attaching corkscrew curls.

What happened to that cub? she asks.

The hyenas adopted her, I tell her. She learned to smile and everything.

A faint sensation passes through me, the girl's relief,
the smell of peroxide and switchgrass, a belief in my own white lies.

Steve threw in the towel the day he gave a man a permanent wave
and forgot him under the dryer.

The man was yelling Lawsuit! His hair wild and seared off at the crown.

You are not permitted to make mistakes, Steve said,
as he holstered his scissors and boar-bristle brushes.

Do not forget that, my friend.

I drank coffee in the empty shop for the rest of the day, circling want-ads.
As the sun set, a draft rattled the windows, upsetting the swept-up bales.

Tumbleweeds of sheared hair rolled along the sage-coloured tiles,
past where Steve and the man with the bad perm last stampeded.

I had to throw something like a curry comb to separate them.

The migration began after I lost my next job – a Progressive Position
in Telephone Sales.

I extorted money for various charities, and excelled at the work,
becoming Salesman of the Month.

The same day, my boss overheard me, on the Policeman's Ball detail,
use the phrase "Pigs in black tie."

I came home with a pink slip.

We drove for a couple of days and Gloria rattled off job training opportunities from her matchbook:

Firearms and Refrigerator Repair, Mechanics, Plumbing.

We settled in a motel by the highway and she had me Draw Pepe, a smiling mouse in a sombrero, and mail it off to check my artistic aptitude.

I answered a sign for a job over on the highway, bussing tables at The Breaker, a truck-stop diner.

Ike and Kyle spent entire days in the lasso-shaped pool while Gloria watched from a wicker chaise longue

in a frilly one-piece and cat's-eye glasses.

We would eat dinner on the twin beds, hot hamburger platters and bags of onion rings and french fries from The Breaker,

watch old movies on the rabbit-eared TV.

I had my big idea the night we saw this one movie about a drifter named "The Coach" who wandered into a Texas town.

The Coach set this town on its ear, romancing the divorcees and teaching their delinquent sons how to stop keying cars and setting fires.

He did this through football.

The worst of the delinquents knocked down gravestones
and beat up his own father.

When he scored the winning touchdown, turned to the Coach
and yelled: I love you, man!

I had a lump in my throat the size of Abilene.

Ike and Kyle laughed and laughed, Gloria began painting Jennifer's nails
with orange varnish as my heart seethed with avarice and hope.

❧

I began cozying up to the cashier at the diner, a single mother named
Dusty who had three daughters in grade school.

They got no grace, she confided. They're about as feminine as bull
calves. She snorted and took a deep drag off her Salem, exhaled
through flared nostrils.

I stood behind her, smelling her lacquered hair,
noticed the Playboy Bunny mudflaps on a big rig, idling outside.

I'm starting a team, I tell her. Girls' football.

She twists a gold hoop earring; I catch the post as it releases and falls.

❧

The Tiger Cubs, an extracurricular football team for girls
between the ages of seven and eleven, began practising that September.

Dusty enlisted her daughters' classmates for me, telling their exhausted mothers that I was a sensitive and kind man.

I seen him catch cockroaches and set them free, she would say, shaking her head in disbelief.

He's a little man, true. But he's built big. This last assurance, smouldering with innuendo, usually got the ladies on board.

Gloria refused to take any part in my plans; she refused to work, or leave the motel room, where she watched TV all day with the curtains drawn.

The boys would fetch her vodka and cigarettes, then run like Apaches into the woods, returning at nightfall with squirrel pelts and fox's brush.

After work, I would drop off their dinners and head over to Dusty's place, bury my head between her legs for an hour or two, then shove off

Her girls started to call me Daddy: I called each of them Buttercup.

I drew my diagrams at night, shuffled the team roster.

Gloria would sniff and say, You smell like sour milk, like something gone bad.

The day we had our first scrimmage my problem became clear – I knew nothing at all about the game.

I had the girls run laps, yelling One, Two, Three, Hut! while I blew
my whistle, calling out Keep up the good work!

At the diner, I sneaked in a few questions, like What's a wide receiver?
The truckers would pivot on their stools, squint and say: Dusty over
there, for one.

They would laugh and hold out their cups for refills: I had been
promoted to waiter by then and was making good money.

The truckers tipped liked hell, and were friendly, if outlandish, to me.

Most of them had played high school ball, their pasts were all gang-
bangs and moonshine,

line dancing in low-slung jeans and pointed boots, guns and ammo,
strapping deer to the hoods of their cars while pissing their names into
the snow —

I took Typing and Home Ec. in high school, flipped burgers at Chunky
Pete's after school and helped around the house.

My mother's drinking got to where she only moved to hurl something
at me or cut out paper chains of children connected by mittened hands.

I looked to the truckers as fathers in a way, or older brothers I never had.
I cut double slices of pie, and slipped them coffee refills, extra cream.

Luke was one of my regulars; he hauled machine parts from coast to
coast; his rig decked out with Hawaiian dolls whose grass skirts
shimmied when he cornered.

He got drunk enough one afternoon to mumble the rules of football to me as I checked out his Grim Reaper and I Love Sandi tattoos.

I was the star quarterback, he said, as his head hit his chest.

The cheerleaders had a cheer just for me. You should have seen them cartwheeling after a touchdown, their panties flashing like phosphorus in my sea of goddamn troubles.

Pompoms flaring in the endless green.

I learned enough about the game to make our practices pass muster.

The mothers who showed up knew less than I did, and spent a lot of time admiring me in my clean white shorts, hooded tank, and cleats.

The bold ones snatched my whistle and used it for catcalls;
the rest made me football-shaped cakes with white frosting seams,

brownies with green sprinkles and candy goalposts.

Everything was going so well that each morning I fell to my knees and thanked God for the love I felt, shooting through my blood

like a roll of black beauties.

For the girls, tearing down the field in formation, a corps of angels taking arms.

Everything was going so well that I threw Dusty over,
shook her off as she clung to me, pleading.

I was glowing as I walked away – I had underestimated her.

The fathers began appearing at the field, a handful at first,
mildly deriding me:

The kicker is calling plays!

How come she sacked the running back?

That sort of thing.

The last day, they all came. And they formed a gauntlet behind me,
cracking their knuckles.

I blew the whistle.

One last huddle! I called, dropping down.

The girls followed, swarming me like bees.

I heard the fathers snap to attention, the rumble of their approach.

They peeled me like a banana, and left me there.

Through my one good eye, I watched the sun go down in the shape
of a Stetson,

brimming, then falling flat.

Gloria and the boys were asleep when I came home,
my face smashed in and torn open from Sam Wood's uppercut.

She had fallen asleep reading *The Bride of Sorrow*.
The boys lay in a V at her feet.

I packed up and hightailed it out the room with Jennifer,
revved the engine and saw Ike stumbling after me, rubbing his eyes.

Take care of your mother! I yelled, popping the clutch
and ducking as he began throwing trash.

I drove for two days, listening to talk radio.

"What I don't understand is how come kids today have such bad manners
They're looking to get smacked, if you ask me."

Ike used to eat with his mouth full, feeding the dog under the table.
Once he gave me the finger when I asked him to stop.

There is fog everywhere: I feel as though I am driving through time
    and space.

The elementary school seems to rise off the ground, the goalposts, in
the mist, look like altars.

I notice that the trash on the seat was Jennifer's blanket, a few of her
toys. Ike had sat squarely on the asphalt, rubbing his eyes.

He used to break out in rashes when I stayed away too long.
Combed his hair next to me in the mirror, like mine.

I want to pull over and find a telephone, call that talk show.

The host is a Christian. When I tell him what I have done,
he will cite something scriptural:

"I know that thou fearest God," he will murmur.
I will press my face against the cool glass of the booth,

my whole body canting in consent.

Operetta

That's what you wrote in some of the letters, Jake says,
interrupting me.

"Thou fearest God."

He is taking leisurely notes, sipping from a demitasse of espresso.

I want to tell him he looks like one of those perpetual-motion storks,
the ones with hats and ties that bob at glasses.

That he not so much sips as pecks.

He scares me though.

Were you trying to hurt these people? He asks, nonchalantly.

I am appalled, and answer No.

NO.

I was just missing Ike, I tell him.

My mind wanders. I am on a bus headed east, watching the stars multiply
into infinity.

I had to ditch the car and start hitchhiking.

Waited hours before a long gold Chevy slowed down
and idled, waiting on me.

Jennifer jumped in the back seat and shook off the rain.

I apologized to the driver, Max, who was conducting
Kinderstücke.

He told me this music was a taste acquired from his
mother, who had taken him and his brothers to the
symphony every week.

Max was from Kingston, Jamaica.

I told him I liked reggae music and plantains.
We drove without speaking for some time.

I once liked this cello piece, I tell him.
It sounded like a crow in a dovecote.

Max warms up to me a little and has me write down
the name of his favourite aria from Verdi's *Nabucco*.

When Verdi was dying, he tells me, the citizens of Milan
lined the streets with straw so he would not be disturbed.

When I hear this piece I close my eyes and see hundreds
of girls in white dresses on a hill, singing in one voice.

I am listening in a valley below.

When you hear this you will not forget me, he says.

I slept for ten hours straight.

Max let us out by a fork in the road and I caught another ride, then another.

I wanted to tell him that I had dreamed of the same hill and valley.

Girls massing like white rabbits in field of straw above the fir-lined alp.

I watch, petrified, as they kick off – a flurry of snowflakes metastasizing into avalanche.

He left me a few miles outside of a farm town,
three hours north of where I ended up living with Wendy.

I applied immediately at the junior high, as a music instructor.

The Country Bugle had advertised "Minimum wages w/Maximum Reward!" I got help in this town, I tell Jake. Miss Lorre – she saved my life.

Miss Lorre was the school psychologist, hired when one kid,
this sad sack with cross-eyes and a limp, opened fire in the schoolyard.

This was several years back: the swing set and slide are still wreathed in flowers; there are candles, milagros, specks of plaster,

letters imploring JESUS BLESS MY CHILD.

She was a plain and sombre woman, who wore dark glasses and a head scarf, long shapeless dresses.

When I began casting for *Heidi*, Miss Lorre sat in the back of the auditorium, watching.

I cast the boys' parts indifferently: the first one to sing "Edelweiss" without coughing became Heidi's boyfriend.

The grandfather part went to a big oaf with a shock of white hair.

Choosing Heidi took days.

In the end I fell for a girl who was sharp enough to plait her hair and carry a plush goat to the auditions.

I placed the rest of the girls in the choir, and had them start yodelling:

Heidi, Heidi, Hei-didi Heidi, Heidi. Hei-dee, Hei-day.

My starlet had a fit of the vapours backstage: I caught her lying in her stage-grandfather's arms, sobbing:

The lines are too hard!

I had been printing out sewing instructions for the choir girls' mothers:
green A-line skirt and white peasant blouse with red braid.

I pinched the oaf sharply and gathered Heidi in my arms:

Hear the mountains calling you.
Meadow lark and robin too — Heidi.

I sang and Miss Lorre cleared her throat.

When I looked up there was a note where she had been.

See me, it said.

As soon as I stepped into her office — a white room
filled with watercolours of wheat fields and haystacks
— I wanted to confide in her:

I wanted to tell.

My head down like a whipped dog, I told her what
came into my mind.

The dream — not of white rabbits, but swans,
lunging at me, bandit-eyed and muscular.

How I fell away, and was lost.

She asked what I was afraid of, Is it birds?

Something like that, I said. Beating my arms and
yelling like a crazy man.

She sedated me with cough medicine and Benadryl
she kept on hand for peanut allergies.

I spread across her chair like a puddle.

I asked you here because I see there is something wrong, she said.
And I need you to tell me what it is.

She never took her glasses off.

I looked into those dark shells and saw a child, crying.

What's wrong, what's wrong?

My mother has not eaten in days. She rages through the
house – the china plates tremble on their hooks.

Her stomach surging beneath my father's NOTRE DAME
T-shirt: he has been gone for months.

I follow her around trying to make her laugh.
I'm a dancing beetle! I tell her, flopping on my back and
rolling my limbs.

She steps over me, wresting a hanger from the closet.
Hand me that lighter, she says.

I give her Dad's Zippo, inscribed Love Forever.

She does laugh then, unwinding the neck of the hanger
and cauterizing it with the flame.

When are you having the baby? I ask.

I have been sorting through my old toys,
thinking of cool names:

Wolfman. Alice. Evel.

Call an ambulance, she says.

She was lying on the bathroom floor; her blonde hair,
fanned out, had turned scarlet.

The tiles were pink-grouted, slick with blood.

She managed to tell me to clean up the mess, hissing
from the litter as the paramedics lifted her out.

My aunt rushed over and found me in the claw-footed bathtub,
holding the towel, rocking back and forth.

Jesus Christ! She yelled, seizing it, and slapping my face.

On the remaining white tiles, a trailing red stain,
a baby with a severed umbilicus.

A girl, still mewing – she marked the towel in a shape I have looked for
high and low since she went missing.

THREE

Jake is impressed – he pushes aside his peach flambé and steeples
his hands.

This will get you off, he says.

It wasn't my fault, I say, forking a wedge of pastry from his plate.
Miss Lorre helped me see that.

Muted violins play as the waiters rustle back and forth
in a rush of red and white.

I watch the bartender mix a dry martini, open a jar of pearl onions.

My eyes water.

I miss her, I say.

Miss Lorre is cradling my head. I know, she says.

I know.

⁂

Gloria received the first letters.
Sympathy cards with raised lettering and gauzy inserts –

He Taketh Away.

We were both suffering.

I mailed her pages from a book of fairy tales:

Hansel and Gretel looking back into the woods as the trees
conceal the sun,

Briar Rose pricking her finger,

Rapunzel's hair falling like a meteor.

Other things I stole from the school's Lost & Found box.

Two blue LIFE game pegs in a car, a hamster wheel.

Some angry notes in Portuguese: *Eu responsabilizo-o. Má matriz.*

Two bare feet, sketched in red pencil.

I was living in a boarding house at the time.

74

Inside the card I copied down, *How sweet the taste of pain when all else is gone from your body!* from *A Stone for Danny Fischer.*

I drew the word PAIN rising in an oven.

I found the book in the bedside drawer. When I flipped it open, a stack of Polaroids fell out.

Pictures taken underwater: leek-coloured legs planted in jungles of seaweed, fantailed fish with deadpan faces.

In one shot, a white curve breaks the surface.

Staring, I noticed someone else's fingerprints on the glossy surface, overlapping, silvery scales.

I threw it back into the drawer, trying to breathe.

I never wrote to her again: I had scared myself.

On the bus to work I thought of my sons and felt nothing, as if I had slept off a bad headache.

The aisle was filled with schoolgirls, pushing each other and shrieking,

their voices a single soprano.

I thought, fleetingly, of my wife.

Girls are less trouble, she had said.

I turned my head as a long braid whipped past my ear,
its pink ribbon unscrolling, and sliding to the floor.

EVIDENCE

The prosecution has an enormous amount of evidence, Jake tells me.
In addition to the clippings, and the letters.

He wants me to go through the itemized list with him, explaining what
I can.

I am staying at the Holiday Inn: I begin to work my way through the
mini-bar, checking what I remember.

– Cassette Tape, Side A: Jimi Hendrix, *Electric Ladyland*. Side B:
  Chopin, *Polonaises*.

– Toothpick box, filled with pink erasers.

– Nylon doll with cotton torso, stick legs. Labelled "The Lamb of
  God."

– Glassine bag containing two blank Scrabble squares.

– Yearbook photograph, Anonymous.

– Child's drawing of a car, by MARIO.

– Gold lamé Barbie handbag, brush and comb inside.

– Pill vial, RX made out to Mr. Snowball, Anaprox DS 550MG TAB.

– Lucite heart in red Cellophane.

— List of twenty-six babies' names, in alphabetical order:

> Alabaster, Britney Spears, Cymbeline,
> Diamanté, Elephant Ears,
> Fandango, Guava, Hellraiser,
> Innuendo, Jonquil, Kingfisher,
> Lapis Lazuli, Miss Ontario,
> Nectarine, O Susanna, Persimmon,
> Quaid, Rusty, Sea Biscuit, Turandot,
> Uranium, Volare, Wishbone,
> Xavier, Yum Yum,
> Zephyr.

The list goes on and on.

I am exhausted, just reading it.

I once had patience, and time.
It was like working on a jigsaw puzzle.

A white plain in a snowstorm.
In the horizon, a red kite.

I explain my list to Jake in a letter as equal parts HOPE and AMBITION.
Hoisting my tiny bottle of Dubonnet, I consider the man I once was.

TOGETHER, WENDY

Whenever I am catastrophically drunk, I am drawn back to Wendy. Before things changed, and after.

Listening to Bruce Springsteen on the hotel radio as I line up my little soldiers. The Boss!

Singing along, *Together Wendy we can live through the sadness.*

I tried this with her.

Reluctantly, she sang along.

Tramps like us.

This is exactly what happened:

I had written a letter to Miss Pam Oriole, a single mother.

I told her that Bunny, her child, would appear to her in a vision.

I was distracted, opening the mailbox.
A car backfired and I must have miscalculated the drop.

A teenage boy found my letter, opened it, and gave it to his parents. They called the police.

The paper ran a nice piece about Des, the teenager.

He lost an eye in "an archery incident" and was a "straight-C student."
They photographed him in a Nirvana T-shirt, arms crossed.

He looked angry. I hate, like, bad people, he said.
He had a complexion like pink stucco.

I was able to get a letter to him, some time later.

He turned white as a ghost.

Wendy and I were up north when the story broke.

Her best friend was appearing in a community theatre production of
The Grapes of Wrath.

I had never read the novel, but I was anxious to please her.
Something had come between us — she radiated disbelief, misgivings.

She was enthralled by the story, even took my hand: I can feel their
suffering, she said.

I got caught up in the handbills advertising:

> 800 WORKERS WANTED!
> TO PICK GRAPES
> IN NORTHERN CALIFORNIA
> GOOD WAGES

NORTH ON HWY 75

LOOK FOR SIGN

Wondering why I had never thought to expand my enterprise:

WHITEWING DOVES

ASTRID THROUGH ZAHAVAH

LOOSE & IN DANGER UP NORTH!

PRAY FOR THEM

LOOK FOR SIGN

The Joads are falling from their truck like flies, afflicted.

I see myself carrying a stack of handbills into a strong wind,
bracing myself as they lift off, against the randomness of sorrow.

Wendy and I hit the arcade and I won her a pink elephant
playing skittleball.

We shot down the waterslide and walked along the pier
in "Life's a Beach" T-shirts.

Later, we ordered moussaka and spanakopita at the Happy Greek.

The rain was falling lightly by then: Wendy downed shot after shot
of ouzo, flirted a bit with Hercules, the waiter.

Fuck off and clear the table, I told him.

Eurystheus gave Hercules twelve labours, I told her. The sixth
was to drive away the Stymphalian birds.

He and Athena shook them from their coverts and shot
them as they flew away.

Wendy's eyes wander, checking out Hercules bending over,
retrieving dessert plates.

His ass in his pale-blue pants like two robin's eggs.

I imagine the streets of Symphalus heavy with snow,
and stand up, shaking.

Wendy runs to the door in tears as I talk to him
in a language I have never spoken.

He backs away, protecting his face.

Glasses break. I tell him that in Greece, this is a form of applause.

I find Wendy by the water's edge, counting thunder claps.
Storm's coming close, I tell her.

We watch waves break in bands, the back of some huge tabby,
below a vault of black and blue.

I hate violence, she says. My father used to beat me
for the smallest infraction.

Like if I didn't make my bed with military corners. When I ate
the 1 off of his 123 Jello.

I smile behind her back, holding her tight. She is a liar:
I know for a fact her father has no arms.

I have seen him and Wendy's mother, parked outside our
apartment, with sandwiches and a Thermos.

Staring sadly, sometimes stumping up to our lawn,
then retreating.

His arms, like the roots of turnips, flailing in distress;
his wife consoling him, her voice low and sweet.

Once, I heard him yell, That thresher took my manhood!

They drive a dusty Ford pickup, stacked with crates
of vegetables, a mangy dog in a red kerchief.

I headed toward them one night and they sped away.

In the morning there were potatoes everywhere.
Wendy acted like she didn't notice.

Walked across this strange Argus every morning,
high-stepping, switching her long black mane.

I did have one poem published, about her.

In *The New Grain*, a literary journal –
it was written in a completely different style,

a style I discovered after smoking a gram of
blond hash.

The poem goes on about her standing at the sink,
the yoke of her nightgown, the white frill of a fried egg.

Then some yellow, sunlight, dish detergent.

In the end she turns and says, I know what you're doing. And I don't
   mind.

The editor called me and said, Whooooo. Cool ending.
You have no idea, I said.

This editor, Thelonius, stayed in touch with me,
especially when I was in what he liked to call "the joint."

He mailed me a raft of kitsch postcards – chubby wahines,
puppies in sailor suits, a first communion prayer – encouraging me to
Keep writing, man.

By the way he wrote, I thought he was a gangster.
He was shockingly profane, and filled with rage.

Other writers, the Establishment, were stopping him from
Keeping It Real.

He insisted on visiting, took a bus across the country and checked
into a motel.

Fucking Motel Hell, he told me over the phone.

On visiting day, I scanned the room until it emptied.

Huddled in the back, sleeping, was an old man,
his face livid with burn marks: Thelonius.

I approached him slowly, holding out my hand.

Books and magazines sliding from his lap, a white pastry box,
tied with red ribbon.

I knew Thelonius, from one of Wendy's clippings:

Elderly Man Burned in Poetry "Happening."

Thelonius Weston, 75, suffered third degree
burns yesterday while protesting outside
the office of *The Incumbents' Review*, a prestigious
literary magazine. Weston apparently set a number
of issues of the magazine on fire to "protest
the state of poetry in this country." While
shouting into a megaphone, Weston stumbled,

85

falling face-first into the flames. His condition is
listed as critical. Weston is the author of several
self-published volumes, including *Off the Pigs* and
Psychopoetica.

≫

Wendy couldn't understand what he was so angry about.
I bet his poems don't rhyme, she said.

She makes an X of glue on the back of the clipping, pats it into place.
Thelonius Weston, she says, smiling. Fucking mental case.

≫

Thelonius was anxious to see my new writing: I told him
I wasn't even allowed to write letters.

He and I worked out a scheme where I would dictate
what I wanted to write, and he would take care of the rest.

What I had wanted to tell Des —

I see you driving with a friend on a country road at night.
Elm branches reaching out through fog to scrape the windows,

the radio caught between stations as the car fishtails,
charging an embankment in a squall of light.

As the police sweep the streets, I will be writing to your mother,
trying to find the right words.

Dear Mrs. Conure. The pain never found him. The fear
made him invisible. Rest assured.

There were other letters, a draft of my manuscript.

Eventually Thelonius was apprehended and shouldered the blame.
He signed an affidavit swearing he wrote it all,

went on to publish my book under his own name.

The Falcon, a children's book, was a huge success: he toured the country,
making a small fortune.

I saw him in the paper, blushing in the company of two writers
he had once expressed a wish to decapitate.

It's all about birds, Thelonius would say. Read between the lines.

I wanted to be angry, but could not. I loved the man.

Thelonius had sat with me for a week straight,
listening to me talk about Wendy.

The shampoo she liked: Pantene Pro Vitamin. Lipstick: Lancôme
Ginger Root.

Happy Meals, Corvette Stingrays, Opium perfume, kitten heels,
Levi 501s, Dave Brubeck, lemon cookies, Chinese bowls.

The smell of grass, sleeping outside, the Charleston.

A summer in a cabin, pedicures, a pink taffeta prom dress.

Sad stories about the elderly.

Why would she collect that? Thelonius asked.

I think she was trying to tell a story, I said. A story about the persistence of fate.

He is quiet as I continue reciting.

The sound of crickets. Flea markets. Sharp knives.

She loves you, Thelonius said. You two are peas in a pod.

He sent her a card: blue horizon, a single slouching tree --

I AM PINING FOR YOU.

The headline read, "Sicko Sends Love Letter."

In the accompanying photograph, Wendy holds my card like a dead mouse.

Her eyes are wild, frightened.

I am gratified to see that her nails are expertly manicured, violet.
The card sheared at the bottom –

I remember the sound of paper tearing, a flash of silver.
I am filled with light.

FOUR

This is the story of The Falcon –

There were many birds in the Kingdom.
They sang all day and filled the sky with their colours.

One day a terrible plague visited them,
killing them in great numbers.

The fields were filled with small fires.

The Falcon, their prince, sought to save them.

He consulted the Oracle, who asked him,
What is both poison and antidote?

The Falcon flew to the tallest tree and stared
sorrowfully at a dying hatchling.

And he remembered diving in the night into these nests,
his talons dividing their beating breasts.

The blood of the heart, he answered.

As he dashed himself against the stones of the Kingdom's walls,
a plume of white birds appeared, singing.

The illustrator gave the birds things like cravats and aprons:
The Falcon wore spats, and had a devilish moustache.

And when the white birds sang they sang, "I'm So Excited."

When I was testifying, the prosecutor would steam: Would you get to
    the point?

My head is in the clouds, with those crazy birds cheeping
some fine disco –

I'm about to lose control and I think I like it.

I was charged, in the end, with enlisting the post office as an accomplice
to "unconscionable and systematic harassment."

I was sent away for ten years. Gregory, my cellmate, a serial rapist,
thought I was hilarious.

He would pretend I was going to shank him with a letter opener, and cower; tell the others to Watch out for that bad-ass envelope licker.

Motherfucking stamp sticker!

Eventually he became enamoured of me; one day he defended me against a gang of bored skinheads looking to stomp me just for something to do.

Gregory told them I was a deep thinker. I had taught him to read a few simple words, explained that in him, violence and sex were like an engine and a key.

I could have been born this way, he said.

Or maybe it was my father shining his shoes on my mother's ass all those years. Whatever.

His face was open, hopeful, as he rolled over those skinheads like a plough.

Through the window each night, the sound of the river, familiar rustling.

Gregory's voice low, asks me, But how do I change it, what I am?

You have to believe, I tell him.

I am thinking, With a bullet. Listening as his breath slows, and the screaming starts:

Come back here you bitch, I'm not finished with you.

Jake was devastating in court, dismissing Wendy as common trash, Gloria's testimony as muddled, hearsay.

He argued that any previous charges were unsubstantiated and irrelevant to the proceedings.

My past was evoked as a motive for crimes he claimed were based in love, not in hatred.

The parents of the children were also eloquent:

My pain got worse. I thought my child was coming back. I just wanted to see her again.

And so on.

I used every page of the yellow legal pad they placed in front of me, drawing small fires, eggshells. Below that, COME BACK.

Wendy did well from our story, became a local celebrity, posing with her kids and shuddering to reporters, When I think of what could have
    happened –

Gloria went on Channel 4 with Ike and Kyle. Her new husband, a marine with eyebrows that met in a U shape, cursed me until they cut
    the sound.

Casual friends, acquaintances called me "introverted" and "a hell of a
dancer."

Gregory kept me apprised of the news, told me a copycat had
appeared, who mailed pages torn from *The Happy Orpheline*, and altered
the text, horribly:

I HAVE NO PARENTS I DIED.

This made me sick. What's the matter with some people? I asked.

Gregory had named his regulation pillow Josephine, painted on eyes
and a mouth.

There was a contretemps: the feathers flew as I prayed, Make it stop,
make it stop.

Jake appeared like a genie, with news of an appeal.
He had uncovered a violation of my rights, which hinged on

Des having opened my letter: a federal offence.

Gregory lent me a tie to wear to court, menaced the
prison barber into giving me a modified Prince Valiant.

I'll miss you, he said, with so much conviction I was
startled and ashamed.

I left him a message that would please him.

Over the small sink I wrote NO.

❦

Jake and I left the courtroom, dodging rotten fruit and howls of outrage.
I blinked in the sunlight, reading placards:

NO JUSTICE, AN EYE FOR AN EYE, *FOR ONLY IN DESTROYING I FIND EASE*

We had lunch at the same steak house. I polished off a thick, juicy
porterhouse; Jake drank red wine and picked at a shrimp cocktail.

I told him I admired his genius: It's like the law is your Stradivarius, I
said, trying to impress him.

He said it was more like a four-string electric guitar.

Losing the thread of these images, I drift off, thinking of hitting the road
with the windows cranked down and The Boss on deck, yelling about
    freedom.

The waiter jostles my arm, retrieving my plate, and I sit upright.

Jake is talking about a bonsai tree he bought his wife for her birthday.

He has tried everything – spraying it with glacier water, feeding it
vitamin extracts, cutting it back with manicure scissors.

Nothing works. Each day, it gets more sickly.

It's dying, he says, abject, and I see, for an instant, his tenderness.

Something small and twisted, failing, in spite, or because of
his constant, anxious scrutiny.

He left me at the Palace, a motel on the edge of town.

As I climbed out he asked me about the other arrest, then stopped.
Forget it, he said. I hope we never see each other again.

He meant this in a nice way: I waved like a maniac as he peeled out.

Pierre, the manager/owner of the Palace, took a shine to me.
I used his phone to make one call, and settled in to wait.

He had decorated the lawn with about a hundred old plush toys
in various tableaux: mint-green elephants on a tiny Ferris wheel;

panda bears hunched around a tea tray;

white rabbits in life preservers, bobbing in a Turtle pool.

What was odd about him was that when people would slow down to look
at his lawn, he would get all riled up and release his dogs.

He had a few yellow hounds he made a show of ignoring:
I had overheard him at night, asking, Who are Daddy's little men? Who?

I've seen it all, Pierre liked to say.

One night, over a case of beer, he told me about Dale, a girl he had
worked with at the Mattress Showroom a few years back.

She was as homely as the day is long, he said. And shy! Only spoke to
me. I used to feed her cats when she visited her mother on weekends.

At the office Christmas party we used to draw names from a hat,
get a present for that person. Five years in a row I got a bottle of Old
   Spice.

One year someone gave Dale a jar of chocolate-flavoured nipple cream
from an X-rated catalogue.

She thanked him, turned as red as a beet.

I was feeding her cats one weekend, Pierre said, and I started poking
   around.

I found that nipple cream in the bathroom, half-empty.

That poor girl had been eating it – Christ, the loneliness.

Beside him, a dozen Smurfs are climbing a ladder. I nod, and we chew
on long pieces of grass, drink beer.

Over the next seven days, I told Pierre my story.
He seemed nonplussed, though he raised an eyebrow now and then.

At the girl and the flowers. Two or three others.

I had to let them go – they made so much noise.

It was like getting up in the middle of the night,
hands clenched, holding a bolt of cloth.

And each time reaching for the latch.

Imagine a quiet street filled with budgies, all named Baby.
Singing from the rooftops on the street where I live.

Every morning we had coffee on the porch and waited for the mail.

An old man, crooked with osteoporosis, would come by,
inching his way to the garbage bins.

He would pick at the contents, extracting pieces of cardboard,
a Javex bottle, milk cartons.

Turning back, he would peer into his bag. Anxiously, like a trick-or-
treater.

I thought of my mother, throwing everything away – It's all poison,
and filled with razor blades.

Of Wendy, pretending to dip the apples into arsenic and caramel.

She once dressed as a ballerina.
At every house, they demanded a Trick.

She wore out her satin shoes dancing *Swan Lake*.

97

I haven't explained her properly, I told Pierre. She sounds unkind,
   cruel even.

When I talk about Wendy, I feel like P. J. Redouté, the "Raphael of
   Flowers" –

I bought his collection, *Roses*, at the local flea market.
Pierre had a stall there, selling hand-painted *trompe l'oeil* lawn ornaments

he had cut out with a jigsaw and mounted on stakes.
Fat ladies bending over, a man's shadow, grazing sheep.

That Sunday I picked up a heart-shaped medallion; a penknife;
an LP of *Take Five*; a yard of pink taffeta and the P. J. book.

The Ladies' Auxiliary was selling lemonade and hot dogs:
I wolfed down six pups, flipping through the roses.

I got stuck on a two-headed beauty, white and pale red,
that has "a fine effect when grafted on the wild rose."

Its history and the express conditions of its growth are documented
   exactly.

The plate beside the text shows a corbeil of blossoms supported,
improbably, by a thin, barbed stem.

Its leaves are deep green and tinged with reddish brown.

The flower floats in white space above its names,
Rosa Damascena Celsiana, Rosier de Cels –

Wendy and I – the rose assumes our strange romance,
voluptuous, unsafe.

One white bloom packed into a mass of pale red, bleeding into crimson.

Limpid petals, a ratchet of thorns.

The leaves, each marked with an intrinsic flaw, appear to be spoiling
from the edges in.

Pierre and I are hitting Day Six hard, with a bottle of bourbon
and Today's Country on the radio.

The flag on the mailbox: *in statu quo*.

Shania Twain is whooping it up as the moon sinks in, settles.

I look across the parking lot at the playground arrangement, the
sandbox and slide.

All of the Raggedy Ann dolls are missing: Pierre mumbles something
about repairs, drains his glass and goes inside.

The smell of Opium, filling room 203.

Sheers drawn, the mailbox in the moonlight,
its red flag raised, shimmering beneath a
canopy of trees.

Spilling violets form a single phrase.

She sits cross-legged on the queen-size, in knee socks
and a black sweater, unravelling at the elbows.

You left this behind, she says. I slept with it every night.

I'm sorry about what I said, to the papers and all.
Lew said he'd kill me if I stayed quiet.

She picks at the bedspread, pulling threads from the marigolds and phlox.
The crickets grate their legs playing "The Tennessee Waltz."

The yellow dogs bark as a clutch of teenagers make their way
to the shore. I go to the window and watch them break into
clusters in the mist.

Let them alone, Wendy tells me. It's late. We were like that
before, she reminds me. She vamps a bit as I wander off to
take a long horse piss.

Pierre washed my car the night before we left,
handling the chamois like he was cleaning Lalique crystal.

This here's a beauty, he says.

1970 Ford Cougar, I tell him.

351 Cleveland engine, 268 Competition Cam, and complete valve train,

Holley carb, Mallory ignition, headers, and quench heads.

Traction-lock differential with 3.50 gear and FMX transmission.

I run some Mickey Thompson slicks sometimes to control wheel spin.

I'm just going to smoke them today, I boast.

Give them TRW forged pistons something to do.

Pierre looks resigned, says, I'll be seeing you.

Pierre stands waving from the porch as Wendy and I take off. The exhaust starts the tiny carousel, the Curious Georges pirouette.

She is reclining, her hands wound through my legs. A current passes between us when we lace fingers.

She is fixing her hair in the rear-view as we make tracks.

The teeth of the comb snag, shooting sparks.

We drive aimlessly, stopping when we feel like it, if something stands out –

A restaurant shaped like a cheeseburger, flanked by giant steerhorns.

A petting zoo with one wire enclosure filled with squirrels.

An art exhibit: "Deb's Exquisite Oils," paintings of flaming skies, pale sunsets.

A drive-in showing *The Corn is Green*.

A bait stand with an automated worm dispenser.

The Leprechaun Arms, a miniature hotel.

Lucky Duck, a dollar store.

A roadside fruit stand, selling gingham-skirted jars of "Jan's Jam."

A cottage with pink gables and shutters – we went to the Open House
and filled up on petits fours.

A United Church rummage sale, where Wendy bought a wedding dress
and veil, wore them in the car.

We pull into the Salty Dawg, a rough-looking bar on the
outskirts of the last small town we visited,

where we loaded up on salamis and cheese wheels, some
Mateus Rosé, a plaid beanbag ashtray, and a carton of Salems.

Wendy had taken up smoking, liked to French inhale like
a movie star.

Inside, a long-haired dude is vibrating to "Kashmir"
while his stocky girlfriend tells loud jokes, like,

How do you keep flies outta the kitchen? Put a pile of shit
in the living room!

Wendy and I sit in the back booth, drinking shooters: I snap
a picture of her: a ¾ angle, her looking at the hills across
the fence.

She blows smoke rings, asks me, Would you do anything
for me?

I want to reveal myself, what I want –

She asks the waitress for a dry Bijou.

The sun beats on her hair through the streaked glass and it is ten shades of black from burgundy to deep blue.

Some nights we park in the woods, sit in the back seat and play the radio. She asks me to tell her about where we will live.

Our house has a big wraparound porch, I tell her, and she sighs, sits closer. Your crafts room is upstairs, and you meet me at the door when I'm done working.

Carrying a couple of beers – there's spaghetti simmering in the kitchen, warm bread in a basket. What do we do then? she asks sleepily.

We just sit on the porch, drinking those beers, I tell her. Before dinner and after. Rocking back and forth, shaking the rafters.

You keep changing the subject, Wendy says. She is spoiling for a fight.

I want to know you, who you are, what you feel.

I am pretty good at ignoring her, avoiding her questions: sometimes I go so far as to sing right over her,

barbershop quartet songs she hates, some new-age
melodies.

Did you want to hurt my children, she asks?

Her voice is mean, unfamiliar.

I am driving past a frieze of barns, a low pink sunset.

I slow down and try to answer sincerely.

The sound of whales rolls out of my mouth,
blue whales, tenors.

Calling their calves as they break the surface, beating their
great tails.

IF LOVE IS REAL

We made a detour and the car stalled. Left it at a body shop and
walked the main street, stopping for lunch and a few necessities Wendy
crossed off a list.

She found a thrift store and we killed some time, trying on hats and
crazy glasses, sifting through the shelves of junk.

She loaded up a cart with filmy-looking fabric, a picnic basket with
cutlery slots, a small, jewelled case.

I threw in some tools, an overcoat, an old wooden box.

We walked to the river, sat in the shade of a maple.

Wendy told me she saw a place for rent.
I was racing a couple of Matchbox Skylarks.

The seeds kids call helicopters fell from the tree.

It was a one-room apartment over a hardware store.

I knew we couldn't stay there, but Wendy kept fixing up
the place –

she painted a rainbow over the pullout couch,
set a doll there, a baby in a blue jumper and sun hat.

What's it laughing for? I asked her, and she pointed out a
caterpillar crawling up his arm.

That's just sad, I told her.

It's beautifully detailed! she screamed.

There were eyes on the bug, antennae too.
The baby went with the place, it was painted a sort of
slate blue.

Jesus Christ, what are you doing? I exploded one day.

I was sleeping off a pretty good bender when Wendy woke me up
cleaning a stack of her decorative plates.

I am nesting, she said.
Very slowly. I could see the fuse winding up.

I folded the afghan and offered to help.

Picked up one of the praying teddy bear plates and brought down
the wrath of God.

Don't touch them!

My hands were shaking.

The hands on the sunburst clock moved like white lightning.

Wendy's lies, the trivial kind, always bothered me – I
washed and mated your socks, I have no idea where
        they've gone –

but I tended to enjoy the others.

She had me in tears once describing a cruel babysitter
who handcuffed her to the bed, and made her eat mud pies.

Later, I found the same story in one of her *True Confessions* magazines: "I Hired Satan to Watch My Children!"

She told me she dated a croupier, a French biker who rode with the Rock Machine,

that her IQ could not be charted, that she was able to astral project herself to the moon, and swim in its lakes.

She told me she wanted to be good, that she wanted the same for me.

I swallowed hard, thinking of comets crashing, creating the impression of water,

the idea of life somewhere close to Heaven and far away.

I'm tired of moving around, Wendy tells me.

Look at this contact paper! She has lined the kitchen cabinets in sunshine yellow,

laid in some pink and blue towels.

She has a knack for seeing the upside of things.

I notice everything else —

a Seurat of carpet beetles in the bathroom sink, the hardware store
owner cooking with pork fat on a hot plate,

Wendy's ass growing like Jiffy Pop, something new every day.

I'll go crazy if I stay here, I tell her, and she frowns over her
macaroni-marshmallow casserole.

The wooden box rattles when I move it under a loose plank.

I hunch over my dinner; Wendy spoons 1000 Islands into the salad bowl.

Dear Miss Swan,

Your daughter's face on the milk carton –

I am reminded of Ingres's *La Source*, the torrent
that flows from the demure goddess's urn.

Perhaps we could discuss the classical elements
of this painting?

Surely Ingres was concealing more modern
principles, or desires.

Or combining them, with history.

Presently I am able to see into the past.

Angela is dead.

Learn to live with it.

꙳

If I had my sons' address, I would send them some pictures,
taken with my JoyCam.

Here's our apartment, that's our cat, Patches.

There's Wendy's foot stuck in a Roach Motel.

This is me in my uniform, holding a Taco Supreme.

These are her kids, and mine. I made this picture
using dried lentils and various pasta shells.

There's you guys, fishing for trout.

These are Wendy's scrapbooks, hidden in a drawer
of lingerie.

The view from our window: a brick wall, a neon M
from MORTY'S HARDWARE.

A rag rug and a basket of cat toys.

Wendy in bed, sick again.

A bowl of alphabet soup, the word HELP visible.

Hundreds of maps, keys to the Cougar.

Darkness on the Edge of Town.

I would include a note: Dear Ike and Kyle, Your Daddy
misses you, and if I could tell you one thing it's that
every silver lining has a cloud,
Love —

These are my writing materials. The box says KEEP OUT. That means you.

Collecting debris as the snow lifts from sidewalks
rimmed in black slush.

Familiar excavations, discoveries.

Another generation of children, unable to keep track
of their belongings.

What is immaterial to them –

Gloves shucked, drawings airborne before countless new
amazements.

Envy is keeping me at their heels.

Like a hound confusing the scent with the fast blood of
squirrels,

baying beneath the tree, its remote trapeze of leaves and
branches.

Wendy rolling out of bed and breathing all over me.

When I'm looking like this, will you still love me?

She is pointing at one of her apple dolls, in the diorama of a quilting bee.

Love is blind, I tell her.

She and Patches saunter off, passing a catnip mouse between them.

The quilt pattern is called SENTIMENT.

The apple dolls are sewing felt hearts onto squares,

contentment plain on their putrid faces.

I admit to kick-starting the inevitable.

Handing over my black and purple cap when I filled
a Lara Croft glass from the toilet,

slapped the urinal puck between a chalupa shell.

Sent twenty postcards to twenty mothers:
STOP LIVING IN THE PAST.

Shoplifted a bag of hammers right under Morty's nose,

left Patches at the pound with some Meow Mix
and a sock to bat around the parking lot.

Started staying out half the night, coming home reeking
of Coors Light and Tabu.

Elbowed Wendy when she strayed to my side of the bed.

Called Thelonius, Jake as well. Wait for it, I said.

Wendy is circling notices in the paper.

There's a barn dance this weekend, she says.
The Mormons are having the bingo.

Oh – the Lord of the Dance is coming!

She catches me staring, puts the paper down.

Patches? She starts circling the room.

I'll give you ten minutes to pack, I tell her, bag my things and walk away.

I wait in the car, listen to the weather report.

Dolly, the meteorologist, says It's going to be a beautiful day.

AND WE'LL WALK IN THE SUN

After two hundred miles of nagging, threats, and tears, I pull over.

Ask her, Do you remember Chomps, the shark museum
we visited, up north that time?

She nods, her face streaked and sullen.

Well that tour guide told us sharks never sleep, that they drown
if they stop moving.

He'd shown us what they found in a tiger shark,
medieval armour, antlers, a dog, a cow hoof,

an entire chicken coop filled with bones and feathers.

The shark doesn't mean anything by it, I remind her.

I just wanted us to settle down, she complains.

In that museum we saw broken cages where they tried to keep sharks,

about thirty jawbones, winched open; photographs of lethal scars.

Wendy is sleek as a seal in her black sundress.

The sky opens like an incision and we press through the rain.

·⁒·

The night before Wendy and I lit out, I dreamed I was in
a major motion picture.

I was a rich industrialist, a collector of modern art and
Persian rugs. When I played squash, I played to win.

I was combing my hair back and talking to a recalcitrant
employee.

Life comes down to a few moments, I told him.
This is one of them.

I woke up and looked at Wendy in the moonlight.

The skin on her face had become slack, her black hair
marbled with grey.

She told me once she was afraid of the elderly, of becoming
that way.

She reaches over and strokes my thigh, and I repulse her.
It is one of those moments.

I am looking for the girl she was and cannot find her.

The landmarks – a forty-five-foot porcupine, sandblasted into a cliff; a beekeeper named Babe; llamas outfitted with saddles and peaked caps –

don't interest us any more. We are putting distance between us, following, with a big red Sharpie, the grids of the map.

I want to show you where I was born, I tell her.

I feel so close to you, she says.

The fields of foxglove start to look familiar,
an owl starts up, out of nowhere.

We are close to home.

    It is after midnight when I find the house, Wendy is tired and asks if it can't wait.

    I want to go to the motel and freshen up, she says.
    Call my children. It's been a long time: I miss them.

    This won't take long, I tell her.

    The old A-frame is abandoned, its doors and windows boarded over.

The yard is filled with dandelions and crabapples.
I kick in the boards, and pull Wendy inside.

Show her the bedrooms, the bathroom.

She is miserable, brushing off cobwebs,
dust motes.

I filled this tub with cold water, I tell her.

She never woke up.

I traded in the Cougar for a '57 Tri-Chevy Nomad, gloss black with
orange interior, spoilers, a four-barrel souped-up V8 engine.

Drove all night and had breakfast in a diner,
eggs over easy, sausage, wheat toast.

Over my third coffee, I notice a mother and her daughter
colouring in a book, cowboys riding through blue sage.

That's nice, I tell her. Mothers and daughters ought to be close.

The girl spills her juice and hides under the table.

I look away, bored by them. In my palm: half a silver heart.

The pendant said WENDY AND —
It snapped in two like a cracker.

Her terror spiked, becoming recognition.

Her hand at her throat.

When I told Wendy I wasn't like other men,
she took it as a compliment.

Women hear what they want to.

I'll wear this chain forever, she said.

Firing up the Nomad, I pull away from the Dumpster
behind the 7-Eleven.

An old lady, dressed in a hoopskirt and Montreal Expos cap, is already
rummaging through the lilac and white frills.

I pass the house where I lived, or something like it.

Toss a letter in the first mailbox I see and clear out.

In the rear-view I watch the sun blaze,
refracting off the smooth black fins.

Dear Mr. and Mrs. Crow,

I hope that your Wendy appears to you
as she has to me, several times.

In dreams, to ask me to tell you to think well
of her, and remember her in your prayers.

She never told a lie.

All the same, I had to leave her.

The ground is golden, there are apple trees
where she is.

She also asked that you do not try to find her:
you would not recognize her, if you did.

Love —

Outside the town limits, I see a hitchhiker.

I slow to a crawl and see she is all of fourteen, with legs like a mustang,
a mane of cherry-black hair.

She names a city a ways over, and steps back.

Don't worry, I tell her, patting the seat. I've got all kinds of daughters.

You must miss them, she says, climbing over my suitcase as I pop the clutch.

Travelling and all.

Keeping my eyes straight ahead, I tell her that I try to keep in touch.

A V of geese shadows us, declaiming the fall.

ACKNOWLEDGEMENTS

This poem is loosely based on an e-mail, sent to me by Malene Arpe, and the first four songs of Bruce Springsteen's *Greatest Hits*. Gratefully acknowledged are Mike Bratcher's Classic Ford Page, Paul Duval's *Canadian Impressionism*, P. J. Redouté's *Roses*, John Milton's *Paradise Lost*, The Holy Bible, Albert Elsen's *Purposes of Art*, Peter and Linda Murray's *The Penguin Dictionary of Art and Artists*, Neil Diamond, Led Zeppelin, The Pointer Sisters, Travis Tritt, Allen Ginberg's *Howl*, and Harold Robbins.

I wish to thank Clayton Ruby for his counsel and friendship; Elliott Leyton, who furnished me with the line "with a bullet," for his generosity and intelligence; and the following people for reading this book at various stages, and discussing it, graciously, with me: Bruce McDonald, Leanne Delap, Michael Holmes, Michael Turner, Joanne Balles, John Bennett, Martha Sharpe, Angel Guerra, and Janet Stone.

I was very much inspired by Ray Robertson, Mara Korkola, Lake Lingerlong and Norm's carnival of plush toys, Marjorie and Nando, Liz Renzetti, Doug Saunders, and Griff, Daniel Richler, Jake Richler, The Wasaga Beach Players, and Wasaga Beach's own Tony Burgess.

I also wish to thank Chris Dewdney and Kevin Connolly, and David McGimpsey, particularly, for their kind assistance, and for their astonishing, always revelatory poetry.

I am very grateful to Ellen Seligman, Anita Chong, and Heather Sangster.

To Jamie Pattyn and Jennifer Febbraro.

And to Francis, my heart.

Finally, I want to thank my family, particularly James Crosbie, with love.